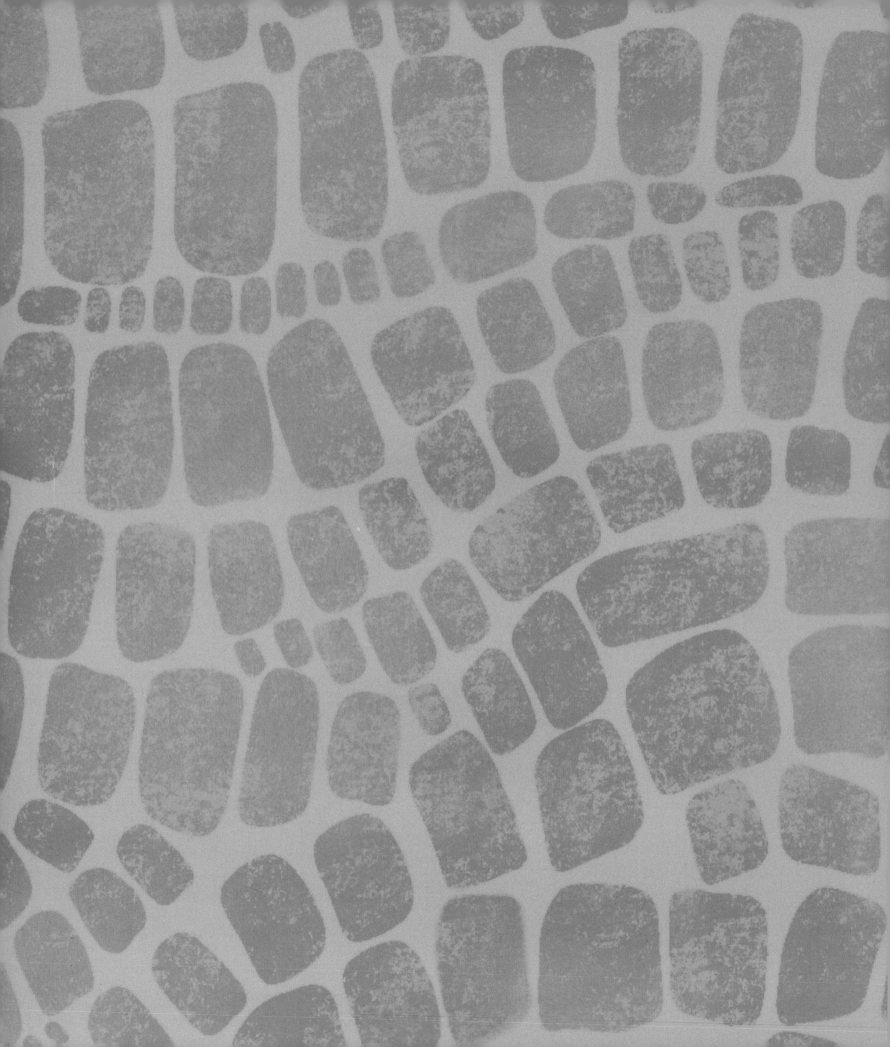

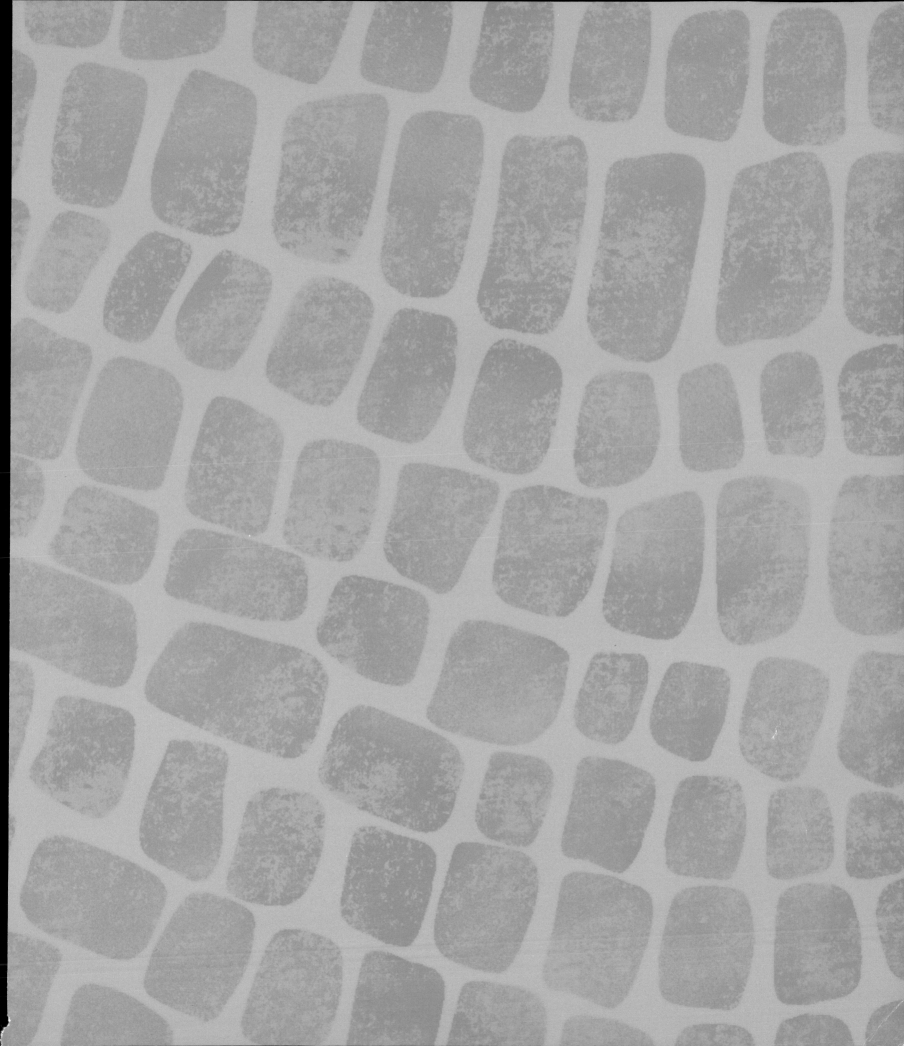

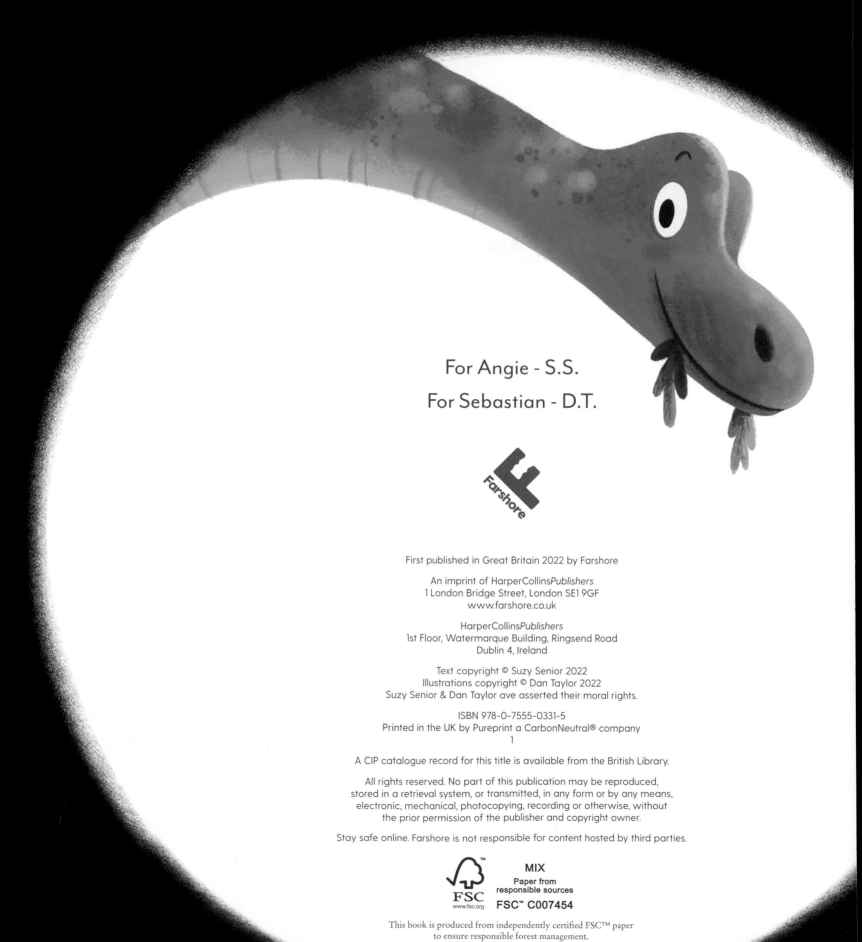

For Angie - S.S.

For Sebastian - D.T.

First published in Great Britain 2022 by Farshore

An imprint of HarperCollins*Publishers*
1 London Bridge Street, London SE1 9GF
www.farshore.co.uk

HarperCollins*Publishers*
1st Floor, Watermarque Building, Ringsend Road
Dublin 4, Ireland

Text copyright © Suzy Senior 2022
Illustrations copyright © Dan Taylor 2022
Suzy Senior & Dan Taylor ave asserted their moral rights.

ISBN 978-0-7555-0331-5
Printed in the UK by Pureprint a CarbonNeutral® company
1

A CIP catalogue record for this title is available from the British Library.

Stay safe online. Farshore is not responsible for content hosted by third parties.

MIX
Paper from
responsible sources
FSC
www.fsc.org
FSC™ C007454

This book is produced from independently certified FSC™ paper
to ensure responsible forest management.

For more information visit: www.harpercollins.co.uk/green

HOW TO SPOT A DINOSAUR

Suzy Senior & Dan Taylor

Farshore

We're off to find a DINOSAUR.
They can't be hard to spot.

They're really BIG and stomp around.
We'll probably find a LOT!

I've got some big binoculars.
My sister's brought a book.
It's FULL of super DINO facts –
We'll know just where to look!

You see! We've found one straight away,
Right there behind the swings.

With feathers and a pointy beak,
And beady eyes and wings.

AN OVIRAPTOR!
EATING CHIPS!

But, whoa – it's MUCH too small . . .

It's just a cheeky pigeon.
Not a dinosaur at all!

So, off we creep across the grass.
Quick! That's one. Over there!

A frilly head, with zig-zag spikes,
Behind that stripy chair.

It must be a TRICERATOPS!

But, no – hang on! What's that?

It's got a **bunch of flowers** on –
It's just . . .

a fancy HAT.

We've GOT to find a dinosaur!
Come on – it's not too late.

A SPINOSAURUS
near the pier?

A T. REX by the gate?

A STEGOSAURUS
in the loos?

TOILETS

OR LOOK – behind that tree . . .

There's something HUGE and curved and grey –

WOO-HOO!

It HAS to be . . .

TOILETS

A BRONTOSAURUS bottom!
Yes! A dinosaur at last!
We'd better get right over there,
And take a photo – fast.

But . . . what?
No stompy feet and claws?
No great long neck and tail . . .

It's just a WAGON selling snacks!
"Oh, let's give up," I wail.

"These dinosaurs aren't
ANYWHERE!"
My sister starts to cry.

"Wait – dinosaurs?" the snack man says.
"I know just where to try!"

He gives us both a lolly,
And he tells us where to go . . .

We find a great
big building.
No dinos yet
but . . .
OH!

I think that's an IGUANODON!
Look, ANKYLOSAURUS too.

A DIPLODOCUS
– wow, that's big!

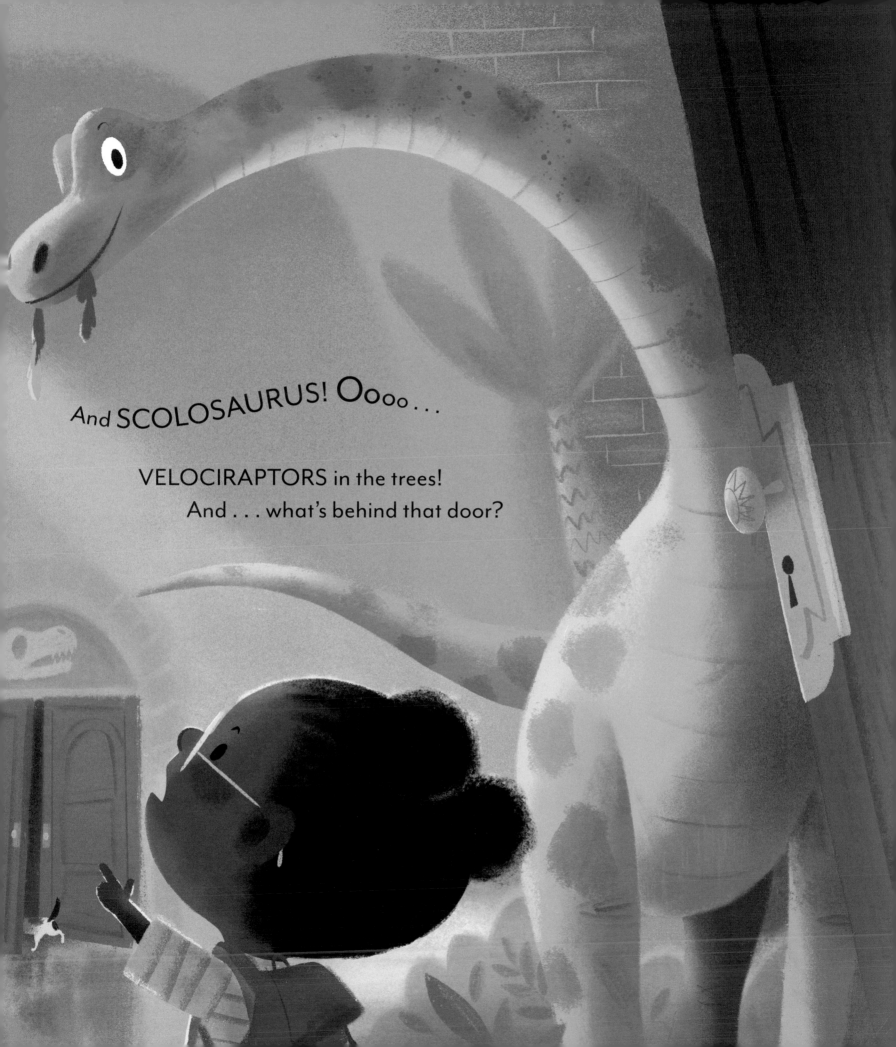

And SCOLOSAURUS! Oooo . . .

VELOCIRAPTORS in the trees!
And . . . what's behind that door?

Oh no! TYRANNOSAURUS REX!

It gives a mighty

"ROAAAARRRR!"

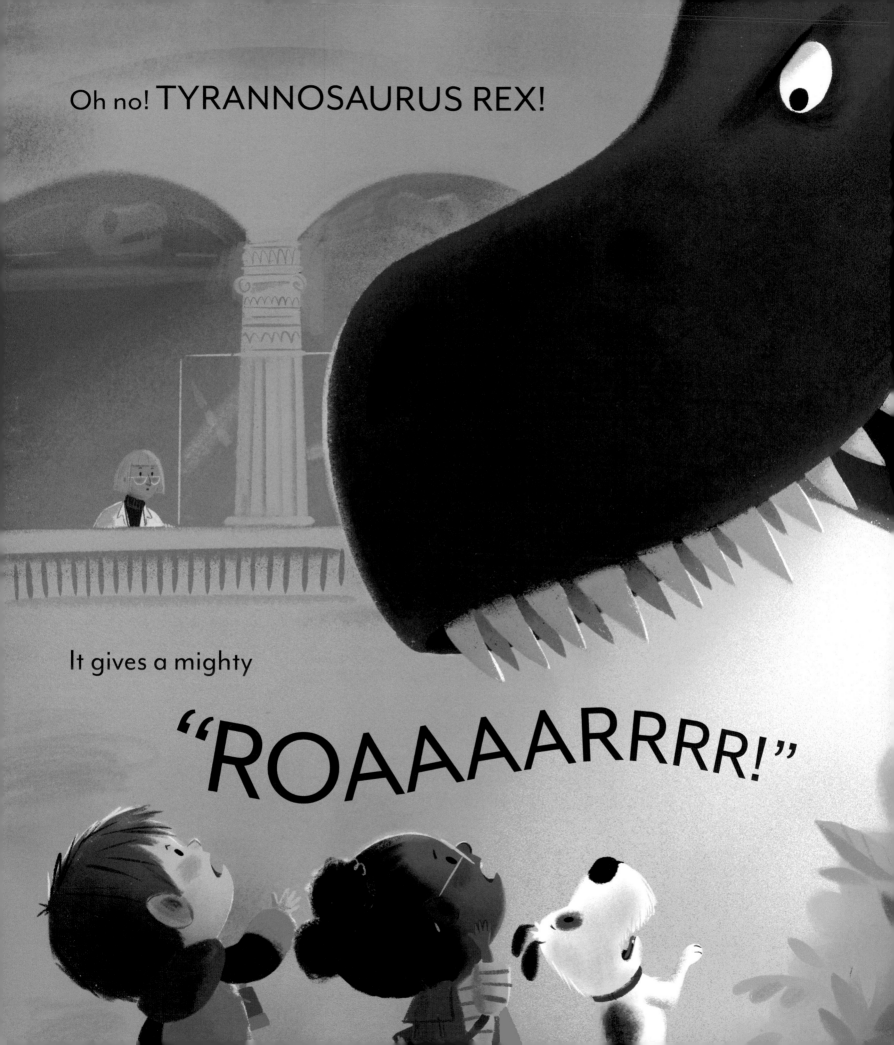

Its giant head comes snapping round.
Its eyes are wild and mean.
I think it might be HUNGRY –
And I think we've
JUST BEEN SEEN!

AARGH! Help! We've found a dinosaur!
We'd better RUN AWAY.
We scramble out past ropes and signs . . .

. . . for 'DINOSAUR DISPLAY'!

And THEN it all makes MUCH more sense.
We won't get eaten! PHEW!
We have some cake to celebrate.
(And then some milkshakes too.)

Then after that, we take a tour,
Around the massive hall.
We came to find a dinosaur –
But, hey! We've found them ALL!

We've had the most AMAZING day,
And now it's time to go.
We won't look out for dinosaurs –
They're all EXTINCT . . .

. . . we know!

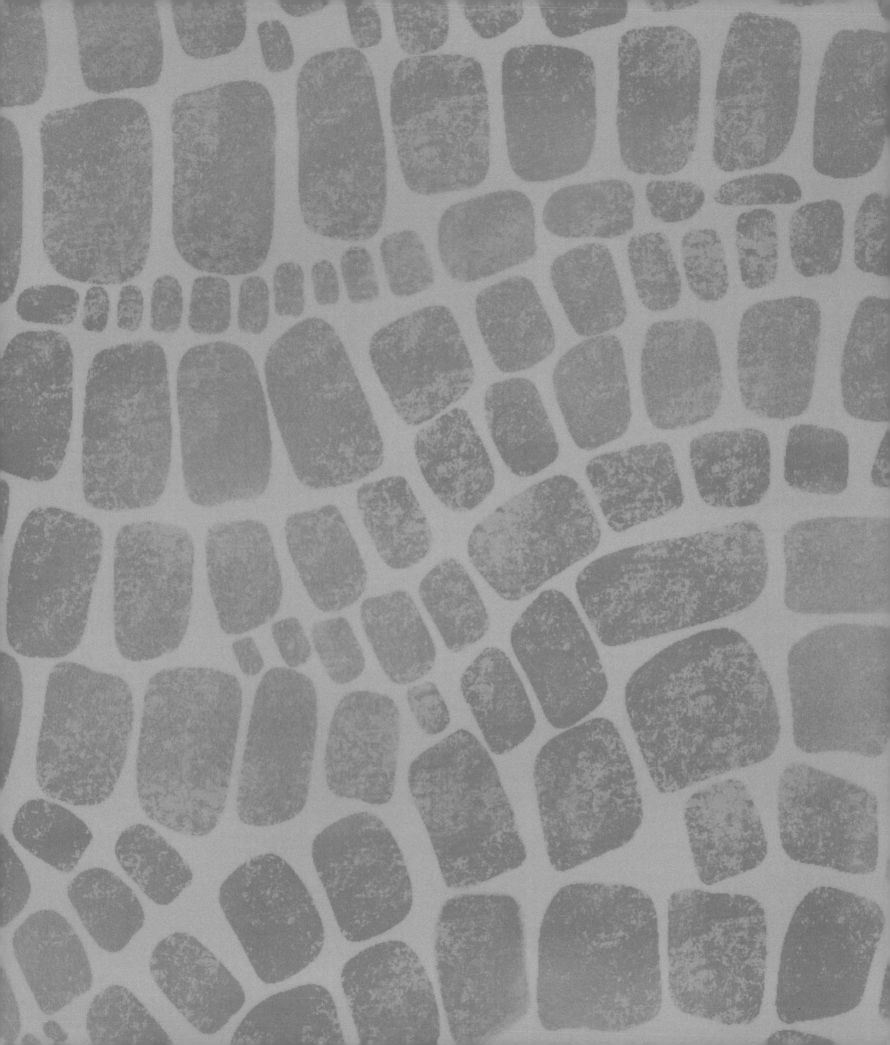

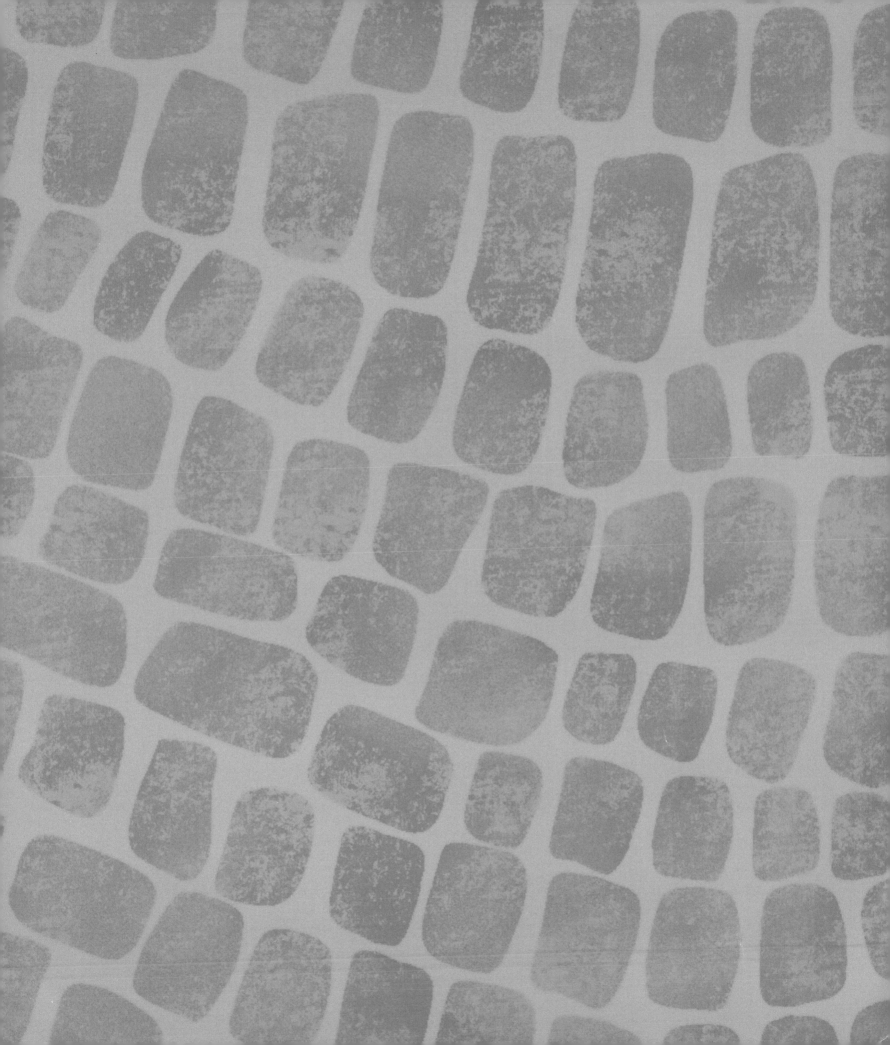

Soon Bear was buried beneath a pile of his sleepy friends. And even though Raccoon snored, Beaver fidgeted, and Skunk was still a little bit smelly, Bear didn't mind.

He was *finally* fast asleep.

"We missed you!" they cried.
"We can't get to sleep without you!"

... his furry friends!
"What are YOU doing here?"
bellowed Bear.

A few minutes later, there was a knock on the door. A man wheeled in the food cart. Bear licked his lips and lifted the largest cover. But instead of a fabulous feast he found . . .

"I'M HUNGRY!" he howled.
"A bear can't be expected to
sleep on an empty tummy!"
Bear called room service.
"I'd like to order the menu,
please," he said. "All of it."

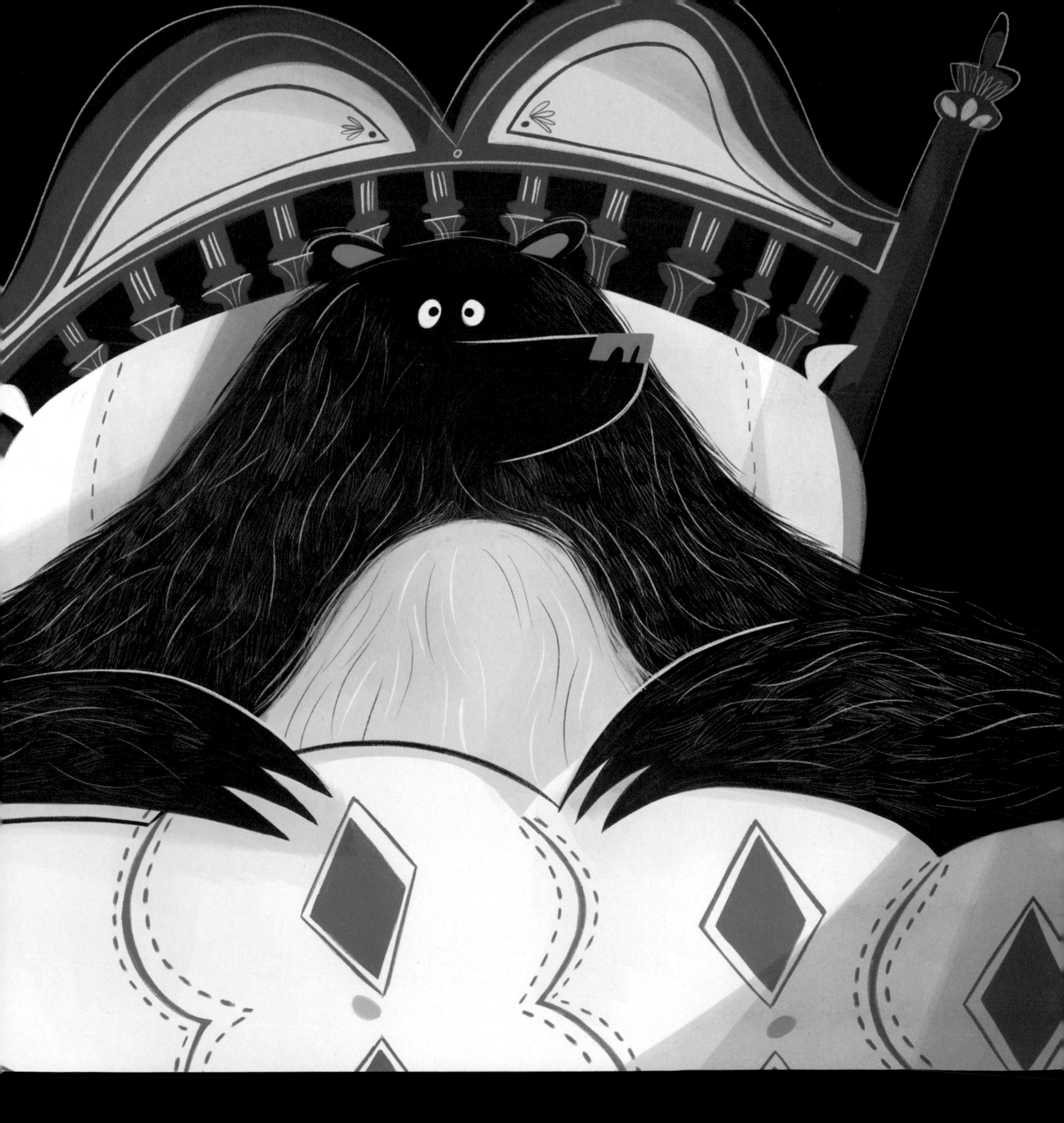

Bear lay in the dark, wide awake and all alone.
"I just don't get it," he huffed. "I'm in a luxurious
bed, with no snoring, fidgeting, or skunky smells.
And I STILL can't sleep!"
Deep in the pit of Bear's tummy there was
a strange, hollow, empty feeling.

And right then, Bear
knew EXACTLY why he
couldn't sleep.

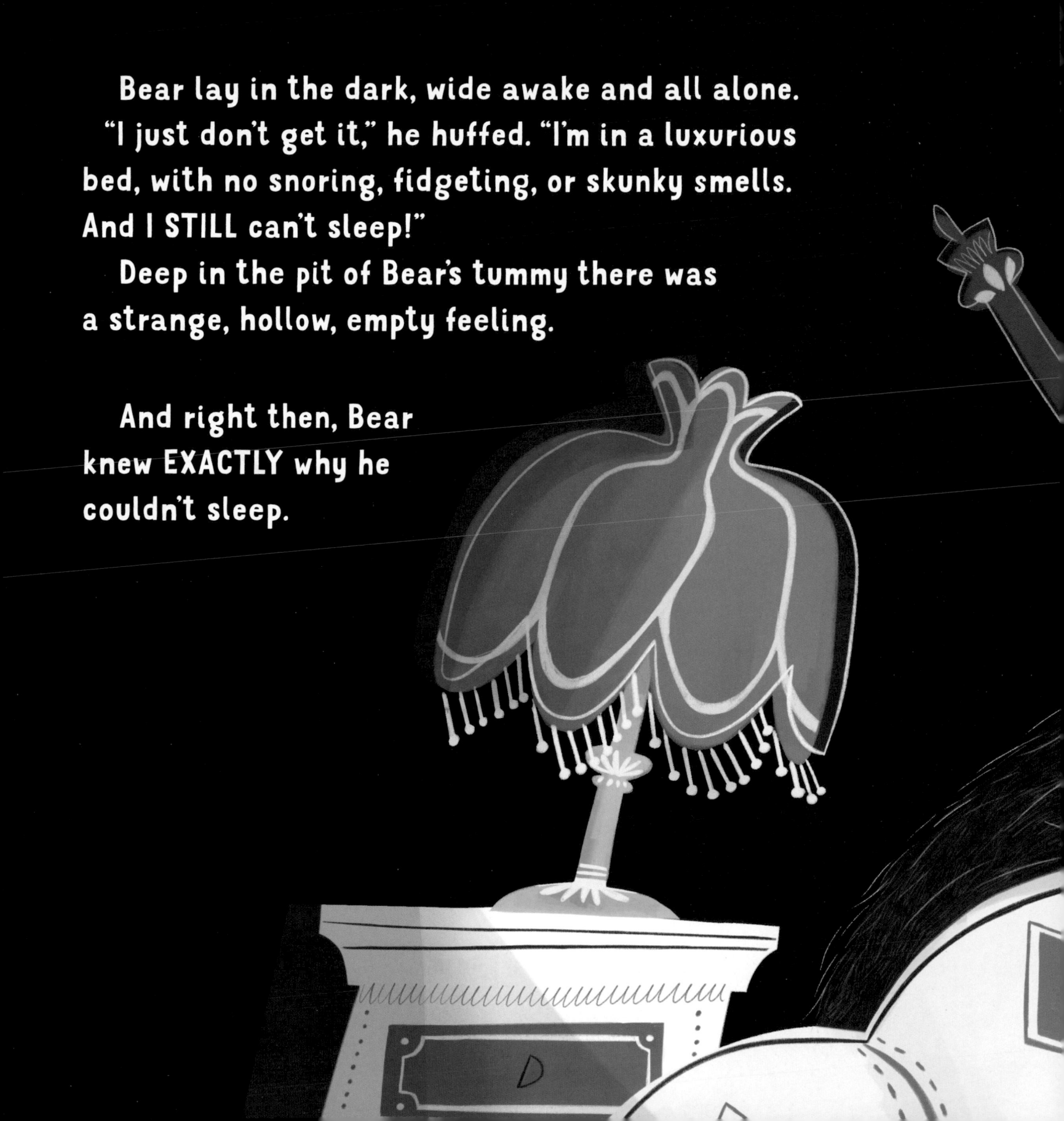

"Maybe a little TV will help me sleep," he sighed,
and began to click through the channels.
There was nothing on but wildlife shows,
and for some reason, they made Bear feel sad.
So he turned the TV off and flopped back
into bed.

"Oh, no!" he cried. "Now I'm too HOT!"
He threw off the blanket and pillows and opened
the window to let the cool night air ruffle his fur.
Soon Bear wasn't hot, but he wasn't sleepy, either.

But no matter how much he tried, Bear just could not sleep.

"HUMPH!" he moaned. "This bed is TOO squishy for a big-boned Bear!" So he flung the blanket and pillows on the floor and crawled under them.

"AHHH! Toasty!" sighed Bear, snuggling in. He grew toastier, then roastier, until . . .

He stomped down the hallway.
"Would you mind keeping the noise down?"
he growled, ever so politely. "I am TRYING
to hibernate!"
The other guests stopped at once.
So Bear stumbled back to bed.

BOOM-
BiTTY-BOOM-BOOM

Thump! Thump! Thump!

. . . didn't fall asleep.
"A party?" groaned Bear.
"This is worse than Raccoon's
SNORING!"

and flopped, exhausted, into bed.
"Perfect!" he yawned as he closed
his eyes, and . . .

Bear used every bottle of shampoo ... and all of the hot water, too!

Then he dried his fur, brushed his teeth ...

"And look at these snacks!" Bear cheered.

He didn't know which one to eat. So he ate them all . . .

then washed everything down with a huge gulp of water.

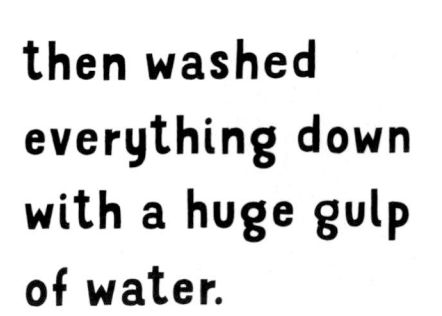

A man showed Bear to his room—
it was BIGGER than his entire cave!
"THIS IS THE LIFE!" exclaimed Bear,
bouncing up and down on the bed.

"Yes, please," said Bear. "March 1st."

The hotel was HUGE and fancy—just like the manager's facial hair! Bear tried not to stare at it as he checked in.
"Would Sir like a wake-up call?" asked the manager.

"Ahhh," said Bear as he drove away. "Peace and quiet at last!"

So he got up, made a phone call, and booked a room at a fancy hotel.

"I've had enough of being treated like a big furry mattress," Bear grumbled.

It was WAY past hibernation time, but Bear just COULD NOT sleep!

His cave, as usual, was much too crowded. Raccoon snored. Beaver fidgeted. And Skunk, quite frankly, was a little bit smelly.

HIBERNATION HOTEL

by John Kelly   Illustrated by Laura Brenlla

LITTLE TIGER

LONDON

To Mom and Dad
~ J.K.

To the best parents I could ever have:
thank you Mom and Dad!
~ L.B.

LITTLE TIGER PRESS LTD,
an imprint of the Little Tiger Group
1 Coda Studios, 189 Munster Road, London SW6 6AW
Imported into the EEA by Penguin Random House Ireland,
Morrison Chambers, 32 Nassau Street, Dublin D02 YH68
www.littletiger.co.uk
First published in Great Britain 2017
This edition published 2020
Text copyright © 2017, 2020 John Kelly
Illustrations copyright © 2017 Laura Brenlla
John Kelly and Laura Brenlla have asserted their rights to be identified as
the author and illustrator of this work under the Copyright, Designs and
Patents Act, 1988 · A CIP catalogue record for this book is available from
the British Library · All rights reserved
LTP/1800/4759/0322 · ISBN 978-1-78881-805-6
Manufactured, printed, and assembled in Guangdong, China
Sixth printing, March 2022
6 8 10 9 7

This Little Tiger book belongs to:

_____

_____

_____

Nita lag auf der Bahre und klammerte sich fest an Mamas Hand während der Krankenwagen mit Blaulicht und heulender Sirene zum Krankenhaus raste.

Nita lay on the stretcher holding tight to Ma, while the ambulance raced through the streets – siren wailing, lights flashing – all the way to the hospital.

Am Eingang wimmelte es von Menschen und Nita bekam Angst.
„Ach du liebe Zeit, was ist denn mit dir passiert?", fragte ein
freundlicher Krankenpfleger.
„Ein Auto hat mich umgefahren und mein Bein tut wirklich ganz doll
weh", sagte Nita und versuchte ihre Tränen zu unterdrücken.
„Sobald der Doktor dich gesehen hat, werden wir dir was gegen die
Schmerzen geben", sagte er zu ihr. „Aber erst muss ich messen, ob
du Fieber hast und ein bisschen Blut aus einem deiner Finger nehmen
– keine Angst, du merkst nur einen winzigen Stich."

At the entrance there were people everywhere. Nita was feeling very scared.
"Oh dear, what's happened to you?" asked a friendly nurse.
"A car hit me and my leg really hurts," said Nita, blinking back the tears.
"We'll give you something for the pain, as soon as the doctor has had a look,"
he told her. "Now I've got to check your temperature and take some blood.
You'll just feel a little jab."

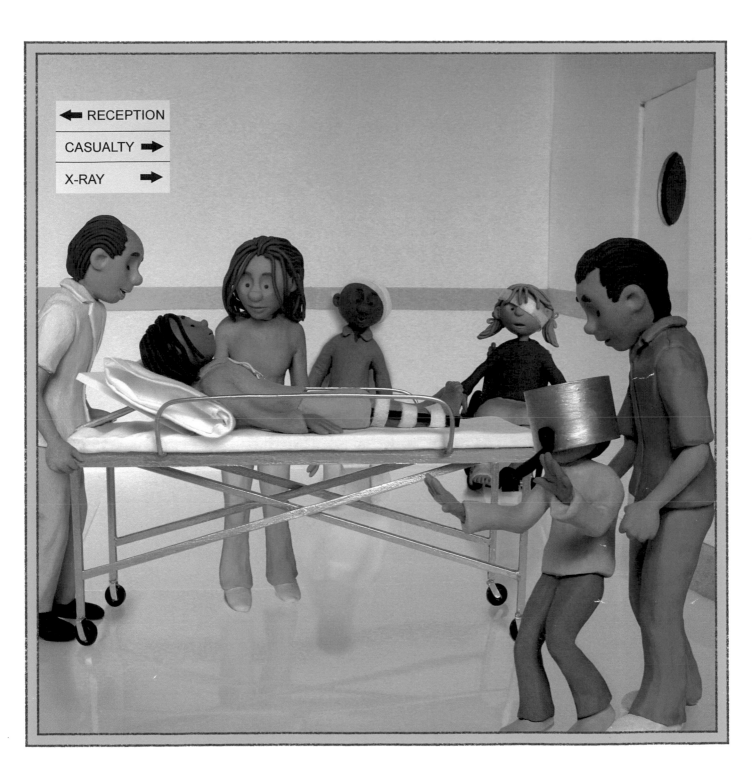

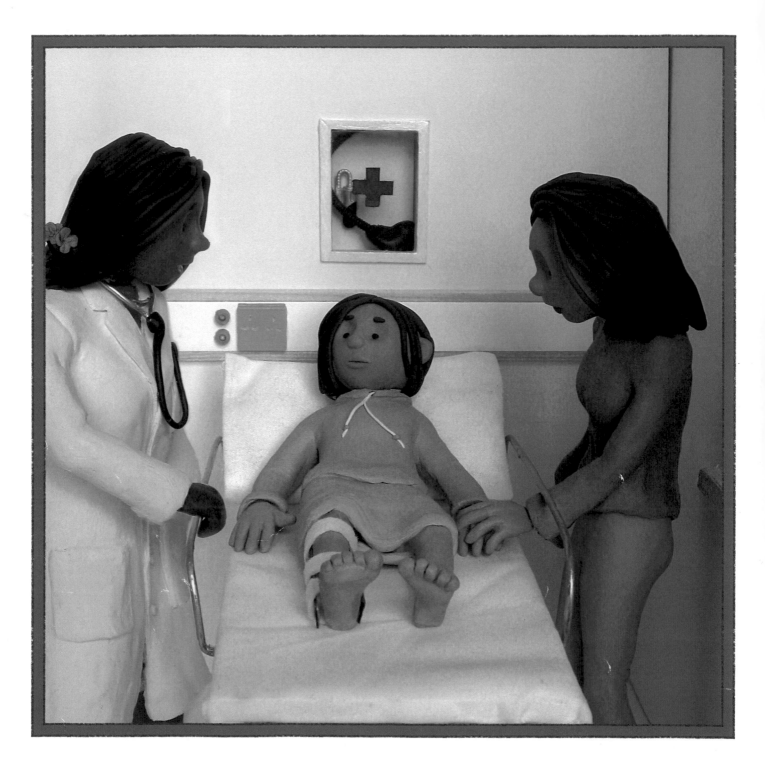

Dann kam die Ärztin. „Hallo Nita", sagte sie. „Oh, wie ist denn das geschehen?"

„Ein Auto hat mich umgefahren. Mein Bein tut wirklich doll weh", schluchzte Nita.

„Ich geb dir was gegen die Schmerzen. Lass mich erst mal dein Bein ansehen", sagte die Ärztin. „Hmm, es scheint gebrochen zu sein. Wir müssen eine Röntgenaufnahme machen lassen und uns das ganze mal genauer anschauen."

Next came the doctor. "Hello Nita," she said. "Ooh, how did that happen?"
"A car hit me. My leg really hurts," sobbed Nita.
"I'll give you something to stop the pain. Now let's have a look at your leg," said the doctor. "Hmm, it seems broken. We'll need an x-ray to take a closer look."

Ein netter Krankenträger rollte sie in die Röntgenabteilung, wo schon viele Leute warteten.

Endlich kam Nita an die Reihe. „Hallo Nita", sagte die Röntgenärztin, „ich werde jetzt mit diesem Aparat ein Foto von dem Knochen in deinem Bein machen." Sie zeigte auf den Röntgenaparat. „Keine Angst, es tut nicht weh. Du musst nur ganz still liegen während ich die Aufnahme mache."

Nita nickte.

A friendly porter wheeled Nita to the x-ray department where lots of people were waiting.

At last it was Nita's turn. "Hello Nita," said the radiographer. "I'm going to take a picture of the inside of your leg with this machine," she said pointing to the x-ray machine. "Don't worry, it won't hurt. You just have to keep very still while I take the x-ray."

Nita nodded.

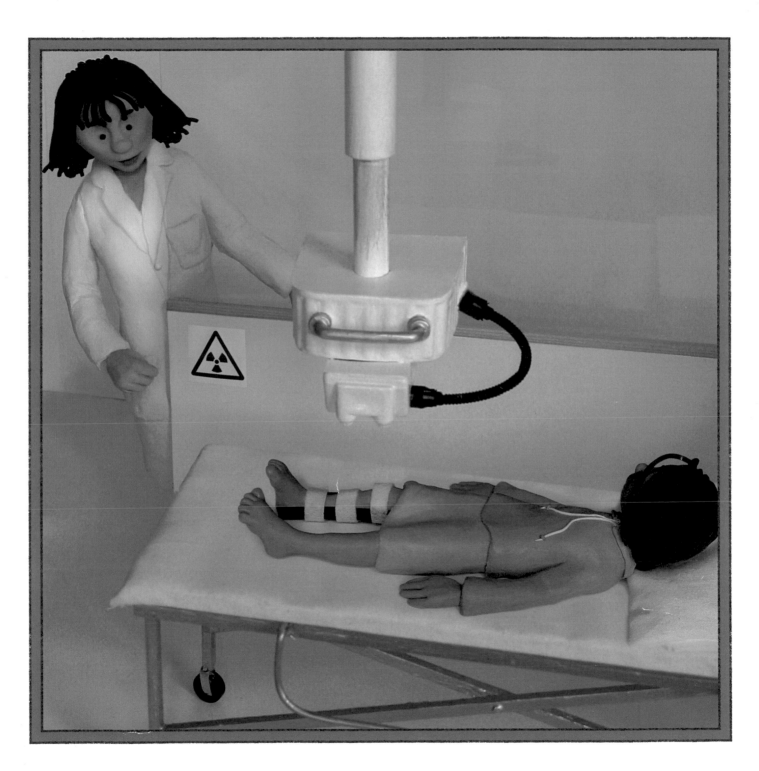

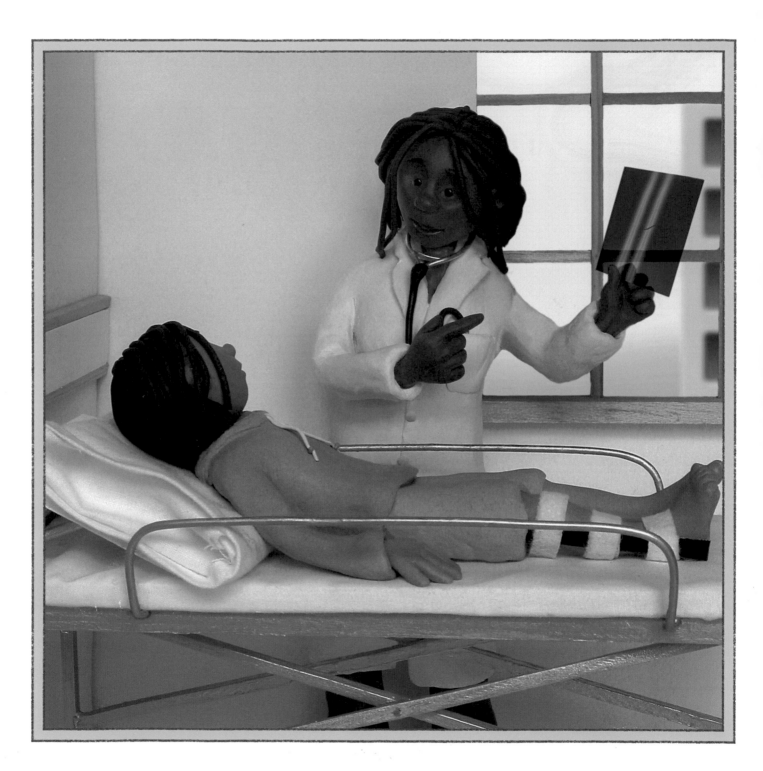

Etwas später kam die Ärztin mit der Röntgenaufnahme zu ihr zurück. Sie hielt die Aufnahme gegen das Licht und Nita konnte den Knochen in ihrem Bein genau sehen.

„Wie ich vermutete", sagte die Ärztin, „das Bein ist gebrochen. Wir müssen den Knochen zurechtrücken und das Bein eingipsen. Der Gipsverband hält das Bein ganz still und der Knochen kann in Ruhe heilen. Im Augenblick ist das Bein aber noch zu sehr geschwollen und deshalb musst du über Nacht hierbleiben."

A little later the doctor came with the x-ray. She held it up and Nita could see the bone right inside her leg!

"It's as I thought," said the doctor. "Your leg is broken. We'll need to set it and then put on a cast. That'll hold it in place so that the bone can mend. But at the moment your leg is too swollen. You'll have to stay overnight."

Der Krankenträger rollte sie in die Kinderabteilung.

„Hallo Nita, ich heiße Rosi und bin die Krankenschwester, die sich besonders um dich kümmern wird. Du kommst genau zur rechte Zeit", sagte sie lächelnd.

„Wieso?", fragte Nita.

„Weil es jetzt Abendbrot gibt. Wir heben dich in dein Bett und dann gibts was zu essen."

Schwester Rosi bettete das Bein in Eis und gab ihr ein extra Kissen, nicht für ihren Kopf... sondern für ihr Bein.

The porter wheeled Nita to the children's ward. "Hello Nita. My name's Rose and I'm your special nurse. I'll be looking after you. You've come just at the right time," she smiled.

"Why?" asked Nita.

"Because it's dinner time. We'll pop you into bed and then you can have some food."

Nurse Rose put some ice around Nita's leg and gave her an extra pillow, not for her head... but for her leg.

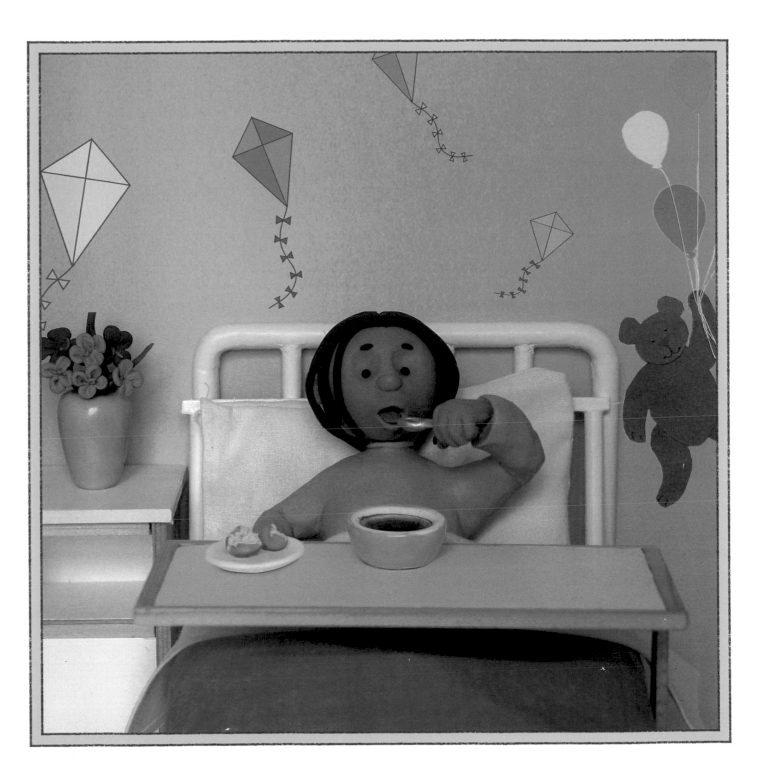

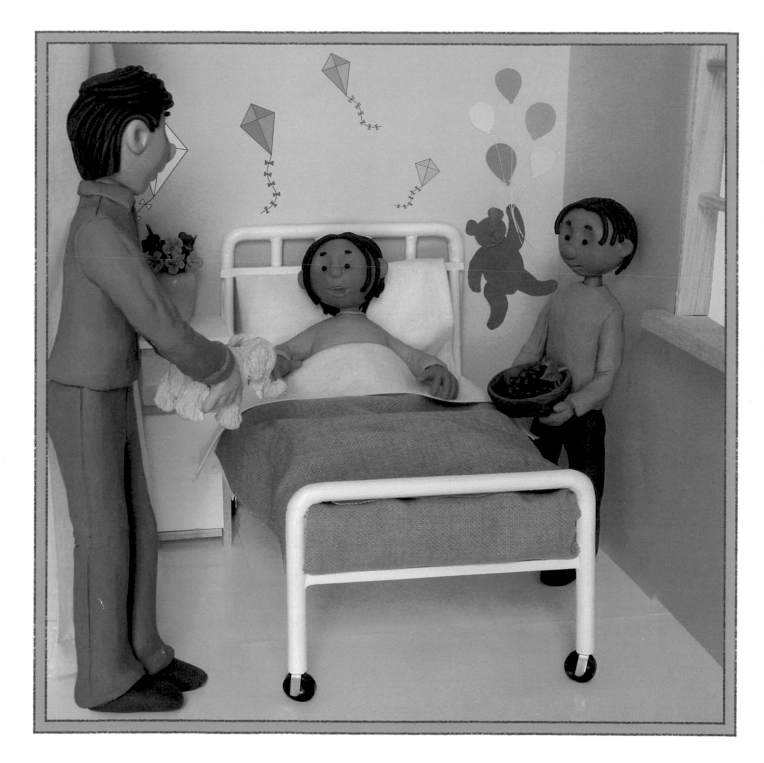

Nach dem Essen kamen Papa und Jay. Papa drückte sie an sich und gab ihr ihr liebstes Kuscheltier.

„Zeig mal dein Bein", bat Jay. „Igitt, das sieht aber scheußlich aus! Tut es sehr weh?"

„Mächtig!", sagte Nita, „aber sie haben mir Schmerzmittel gegeben." Schwester Rosi kam, um noch mal Nitas Temperatur zu messen, „Zeit zu schlafen", sagte sie. „Papa und Jay müssen jetzt gehen, aber Mama kann die ganze Nacht hierbleiben."

After dinner Dad and Jay arrived. Dad gave her a big hug and her favourite toy.

"Let's see your leg?" asked Jay. "Ugh! It's horrible. Does it hurt?"

"Lots," said Nita, "but they gave me pain-killers."

Nurse Rose took Nita's temperature again. "Time to sleep now," she said.

"Dad and your brother will have to go but Ma can stay... all night."

Früh am nächten Morgen kam die Ärztin, um Nitas Bein anzuschauen. „Gut, das sieht viel besser aus", sagte sie, „ich denke, wir können den Knochen jetzt einrichten."

„Was bedeutet das?", fragte Nita.

„Wir geben dir eine Betäubung, die dich einschlafen lässt. Und dann bringen wir den Knochen wieder in die genau richtige Lage und legen dir einen Gipsverband an, der den Knochen in dieser Lage hält bis er geheilt ist. Du brauchst keine Angst zu haben, du wirst von all dem überhaupt nichts merken", sagte die Ärztin.

Early next morning the doctor checked Nita's leg. "Well that looks much better," she said. "I think it's ready to be set."

"What does that mean?" asked Nita.

"We're going to give you an anaesthetic to make you sleep. Then we'll push the bone back in the right position and hold it in place with a cast. Don't worry, you won't feel a thing," said the doctor.

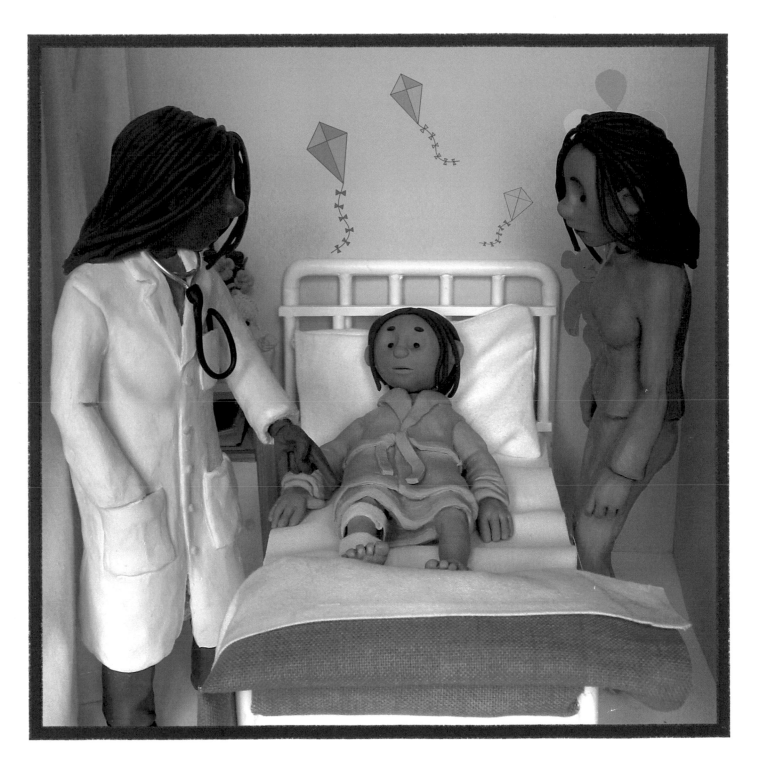

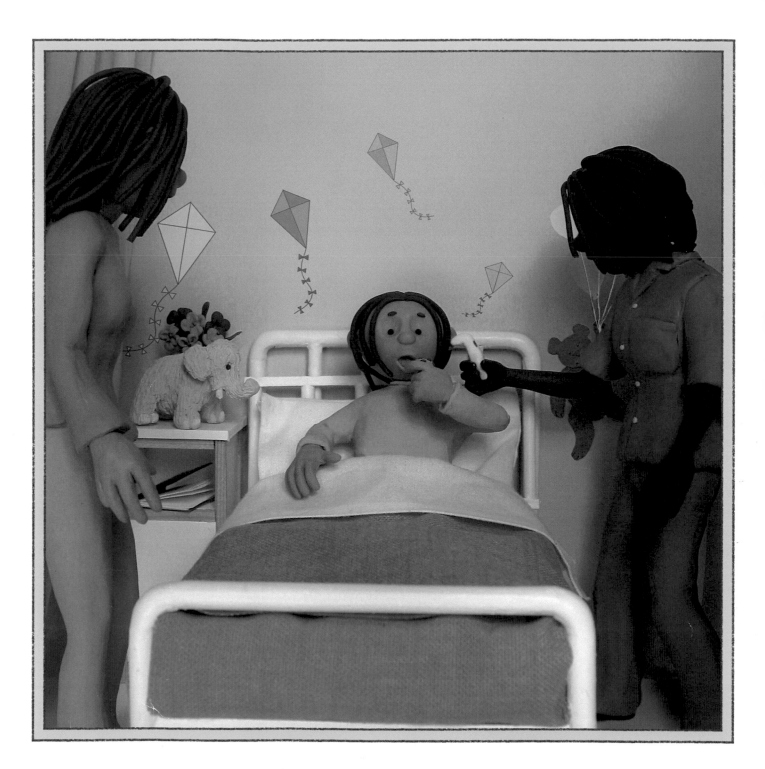

Nita fühlte sich als hätte sie eine Woche lang geschlafen. „Wie lange hab ich denn geschlafen, Mama?", fragte sie.

„Nur etwa eine Stunde", lächelte Mama.

„Hallo Nita", sagte Schwester Rosi, „schön, dich wieder wach zu sehen. Wie gehts dem Bein?"

„OK, aber es fühlt sich furchtbar schwer und steif an", sagte Nita. „Kann ich was zu essen haben?"

„Ja, bald, es ist schon fast Mittag", sagte Rosi.

Nita felt like she'd been asleep for a whole week. "How long have I been sleeping, Ma?" she asked.

"Only about an hour," smiled Ma.

"Hello Nita," said Nurse Rose. "Good to see you've woken up. How's the leg?"

"OK, but it feels so heavy and stiff," said Nita. "Can I have something to eat?"

"Yes, it'll be lunchtime soon," said Rose.

Als es Mittag war, fühlte Nita sich schon viel besser. Schwester Rosi setzte sie in einen Rollstuhl, damit sie mit den andern Kindern am Tisch essen konnte.

„Was hast du denn?", fragte ein Junge.

„Ein gebrochnes Bein", antwortete Nita. „Und du?"

„Mich haben sie an den Ohren operiert", sagte der Junge.

By lunchtime Nita was feeling much better. Nurse Rose put her in a wheelchair so that she could join the other children.

"What happened to you?" asked a boy.

"Broke my leg," said Nita. "And you?"

"I had an operation on my ears," said the boy.

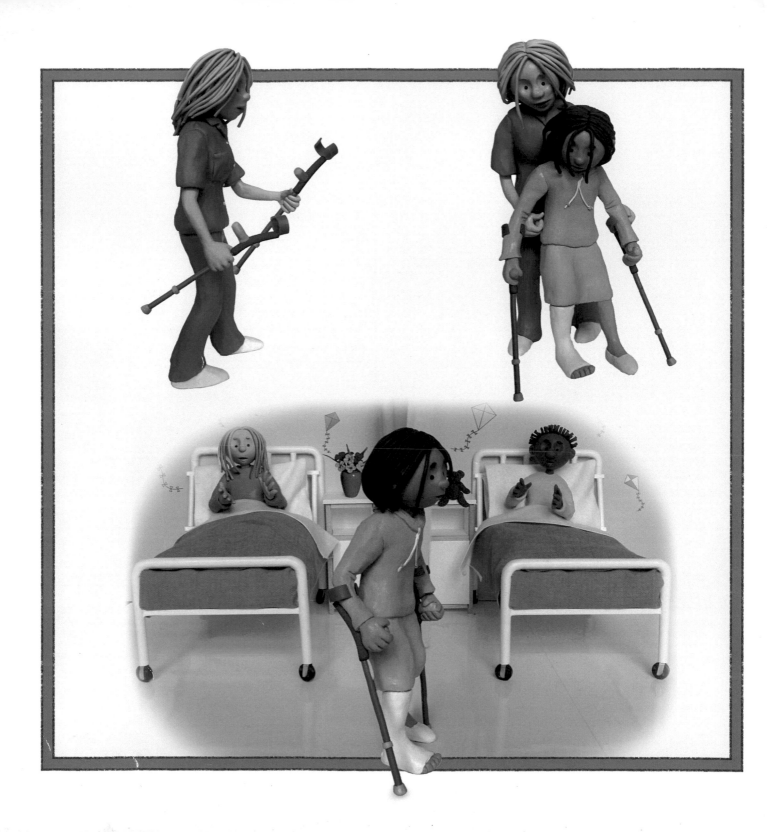